1980

Hefter
Buttons

JAN. 24 1981	DATE DUE	
FEB. 1 4 1981	MAY 2 1 1983	
MAR. 5 1981	OCT. 2 2 1984	
MAR. 2 1 1981	NOV. 8 1984	
	SEP. 2 0 1988	
OCT. 1 9 1981	JUL 3 1 1989	
FEB. 2 7 1982	MAY 0 6 1991	
MAY 3 1982	NOV. 0 2 1992	
MAY 3 1 1982	NOV. 0 5 1992	
	NOV. 2 8 1992	
JAN. 2 2 1983		

THIS

SWEET PICKLES ®

BOOK
BELONGS TO

In the world of *Sweet Pickles,* each animal gets into a pickle because of an all too human personality trait.

This book is about Moody Moose. You never know just what mood he's going to be in next.

Other Books in the Sweet Pickles Series

Library of Congress Cataloging in Publication Data

Hefter, Richard.
  Moody Moose buttons.

  (Sweet Pickles series)
  SUMMARY: Nobody knows what mood Moose will be in
next, until Zebra dreams up a special present.
  [1. Moose—Fiction] I. Title. II. Series.
PZ7.H3587Mo   [E]   77-7255
ISBN 0-03-021446-7

SWEET PICKLES is the registered trademark of
Perle/Reinach/Hefter.

Printed in the United States of America

Weekly Reader Books' Edition

Weekly Reader Books presents

MOODY MOOSE BUTTONS

Written and Illustrated
by Richard Hefter
Edited by Ruth Lerner Perle

Holt, Rinehart and Winston · New York

Zebra was having a special party and Alligator was the first to arrive.

"I knew it!" said Alligator. "Everybody's late!"

"Not at all," answered Zebra. "You're early."

"Well, it's your fault," snarled Alligator. "You should have put the time on the invitations."

"But I didn't send any invitations," smiled Zebra. "That's your fault, too!" screeched Alligator. "And anyway, how will folks know they're invited if you didn't send invitations?"

"Oh, I never send invitations to a party," giggled Zebra. "Whenever I want to give a party, I just tell Yak about it. Yak tells it around town and pretty soon everyone shows up."

"That's terrible," grumbled Alligator. "What about the ones you don't want to come to your party?"

"I always want everybody to come to my parties," laughed Zebra. "That's what parties are for!"

"What about the ones you don't like?" said Alligator.

"I like everyone," chuckled Zebra, "even the ones I don't like."

"You're nuts!" mumbled Alligator.

Elephant and Rabbit came trotting through the garden. They were carrying Goose.

"Hi, Zebra," called Elephant. "Heard you were having a party. Can we come?"

"Why, sure," smiled Zebra. "Everyone's invited."

"We brought Goose along," called Rabbit. "But she fell asleep on the way."

"I'll get her something to eat," said Elephant. "That will wake her up."

Kangaroo and Lion arrived next. Vulture and
Nightingale came too.

Pretty soon almost everybody was there.

"Zebra is nuts to invite everybody," complained Alligator. "Someone is sure to come and spoil this party."

"I doubt that," said Dog.

"Oh, yeah!" smirked Alligator. "What about Moose? If he shows up, that will be the end of this party. He's so moody, he can ruin any party."

"He's probably in a bad mood and won't even come," said Dog.

"But if he does," frowned Alligator, "he'll spoil everything. One minute he's laughing his head off. The next minute he's crying his eyes out!"

"True," said Dog. "You never know what he's going to do next. I never know what to say to him."

"That's what I mean," nodded Alligator. "If Moose turns up, he'll ruin the party and it's Zebra's fault!"

Just then, Moose walked into the garden. He heaved a heavy sigh.

"I knew it!" screamed Alligator." It's Zebra's fault!"

Zebra jumped up on the table. "Listen, everybody," he called. "The guest of honor has arrived. Every party has a reason and the reason for this party is Moose. This is a MOOSEDAY party!"

Moose started to laugh and laugh and laugh.
Everyone laughed with him.

Then, all of a sudden, he began to cry.
Everyone looked at him.
"If I had only known," sobbed Moose, "I would have worn my good suit!"

"Oh, dear," said everybody. "What do we do now?"
Suddenly Moose began to laugh again. "Never mind.
It's all right. My good suit is at the cleaners anyway."
And then he began to cry again.
"You wouldn't catch me crying if this were an
Alligatorday party!" grumbled Alligator.
"I heard that, you nasty Alligator!" screamed Moose.
"And I'll get you for it!"

Moose started to chase Alligator around the table. "Stand still, you dunderhead!" he yelled. "I'll bop you right on your snout!"

"Help!" squawked Alligator. "Mad Moose!"

Alligator slid under the table and bumped right into
Goose who was resting there. The ice cream cake fell
off the table and landed with a plop...right on
Alligator's head.

"Whoops!" giggled Moose. "You sure do look funny." And he started to laugh. He laughed and laughed so hard that he fell right on top of Alligator. Then he began to cry. "I'm sorry, Alligator," he sobbed. "I'm so sorry if I hurt you. I'm so very, very, sorry."

"You picked a fine time to tell me," growled Alligator. "Just look at this mess and it's all your fault!"

"I know!" wailed Moose. "It's always all my fault. Why can't I ever do anything right?"
Moose cried and sniffled and howled.

"Hold on there, Moose," called Zebra. "We can't have the guest of honor crying at a Mooseday party. Besides, you didn't do anything wrong. You're just moody and that's okay. But sometimes we get mixed up because we don't know what mood to expect. And that's why we have a special present for you!"

"You do?" smiled Moose. "What is it?"

"MOODY MOOSE BUTTONS!" laughed Zebra.

"What are Moody Moose Buttons?" asked Moose.

"These are!" said Zebra, holding up two big round yellow buttons. One had a big sweet smile on it. The other had a big sour frown.

"Listen!" said Zebra. "When you're in a *good* mood, you wear the sweet button. When you're in a *bad* mood, you wear the sour button.

"That way, when we see the sweet button we can all say, 'Hi, there, Moose. Great day, isn't it?' And when we see the sour button, we can all say, 'Oh, dear! Poor Moose! How can we help you?'"

"That's wonderful!" said Moose gaily. "I'll try them right now." He took the Moody Moose Buttons and ran into the house.

"You have to admit it, Alligator," said Dog, "sometimes that Zebra gets great ideas."

"Well, I'll tell you one thing," said Alligator, "if I ever see that sour button on Moose, I'm going the other way...fast!"

"Look!" said Dog. "Here comes Moose now!"

Moose was walking out of the house, wearing the big sweet smile button.

"Thank goodness!" cried Elephant. "Moose is in a good mood!"

"Hooray!" shouted everybody.
Then Moose took out a large handkerchief
and began to cry.

"Wait a minute," called Zebra. "You're wearing your sweet button. You're supposed to be in a good mood! Why are you crying, Moose?"

"I can't help it," sniffled Moose. "Nobody has ever given me a Mooseday party before. I'm crying because I'm so happy!"

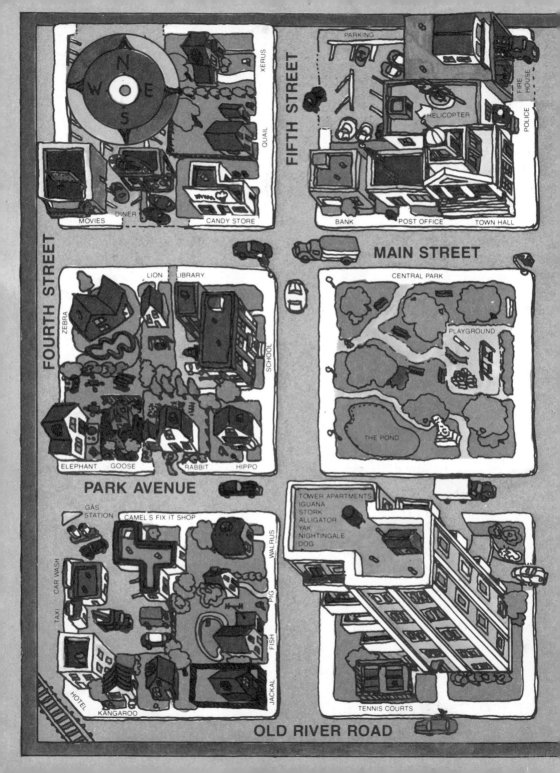